BE TIDY, OR NOT?

Zoom-Boom Book Series

By Joel Brown

Illustrated by
Garrett Myers

Rapier Kids
A Division of Rapier Publishing Company

BE TIDY, OR NOT?
Copyright © 2015

By Joel Brown
Illustrated by Garrett Myers

ISBN 978-0-9966083-2-9
Library of Congress Control Number 2015948180

Published by
Rapier Publishing Company
260 W. Main Street, Suite #1
Dothan, Alabama 36301

www.rapierpublishing.com
Facebook: www.rapierpublishing@gmail.com
Twitter: rapierpublishing@rapierpub

Book Cover Design: Garrett Myers/ Book Layout: Rapture Graphics

Follow all the Current Zoom-Boom Book Series by Joel Brown:

Zoom-Boom the Scarecrow and Friends
Be Tidy, or Not?
Be Careful

Thank you for buying this book. It is important to me that my stories are humorous and educational for the adults and children that read them. I was God-inspired to write the Zoom-Boom series of books for my granddaughters. I wanted the stories to be read mainly at bedtime, so that the time shared during those moments would invite questions from the children and discussions about the stories with the parents. I wanted children to have happy thoughts and dreams at bedtime and what better way to do that than to have the comfort and love of a parent reading a *"Zoom-Boom"* bedtime story. With such busy schedules, we often miss opportunities to make our children feel safe and secure while they are awake. So, a soothing voice, a bedtime story, a hug and a kiss before going to sleep is a wonderful way to end the day. This way, the children can feel that *Zoom-Boom* can handle any "Green Eyed Monster" that might be hiding under the bed or in the closet, should they awaken during the night after a nightmare. I hope that you and your children will enjoy reading these stories, as much as I enjoyed writing them.

Author
Joel Brown

BE TIDY, OR NOT?

It's a typical kind of day on the farm and...

...it's time to do the chores around the house!

Everyone is different and that is very true of "Dirty Bird" and "Charm."

DIRTY:

1. NOT CLEAN
2. SMELLS BAD
3. UN-TIDY
4. MESSY
5. DOESN'T LIKE SOAP
6. JUNKY
7. NOT NEAT
8. FILTHY
9. UGH!

Each of them is quite the opposite of their names.

CHARMING:

1. CLEAN
2. SMELLS GOOD
3. TIDY
4. NOT MESSY
5. LIKES SOAP
6. NOT JUNKY
7. NEAT
8. NOT FILTHY
9. NOT UGH!

Dirty Bird is not "dirty" at all!
In fact, he is neat, clean and has a very tidy home.
Dirty Bird gets up every morning and makes up his bed first.
Do you make up your bed boys and girls?

Dirty Bird also takes a shower with soap and water.
He washes his face and brushes his teeth.
He wants to make sure that he isn't
a "dirty bird!"

He takes his clothes out of his neatly arranged closet
and he always picks up his toys and other items that he uses.
He never leaves home for school, unless his room is tidy!

His floor is so clean that he could use it as a mirror.
His walls are nicely painted and there is no dust to be found
on his furniture or pictures.

Dirty Bird said that being tidy is easy,
because when he is tidy,
he knows where everything is in his home!

And then, there is "Charm." Oh dear, is she messy!
Charm never makes up her bed,
and she only takes a bath or shower
when she wants to, which is not very often. Phew!

Her clothes and her toys are scattered everywhere,
and her floors are never clean. Charm can never find anything,
because she doesn't know where to begin to look!

Being untidy is easy for her too,

because she doesn't have to do anything!

Charm never knows where anything is!

It's in her house somewhere,

but where?

Yes, Dirty Bird is neat and tidy.

And Charm is messy and unclean!

They are so very different from each other.

But you know what?

They are still friends.

Being different doesn't

mean that you can't be friends!

Just because Dirty Bird is neat and tidy,
it doesn't make him "better"
than Charm!

And just because Charm is messy and unclean,
it should not make her feel sad!

We have to accept everyone

just as they are!

You may not "like" that someone is neat and tidy

and you are not.

And they should not dislike you

because you are messy and unclean!

Charm and Dirty Bird found something that they both "like" about each other. They both like to read books! They share books and Charm always makes sure that she takes good care of her books, because she wants Dirty Bird to read them.

And when she returns a book that Dirty Bird has given to her to read, she makes sure it has not been torn or dirty.
She keeps her books in a "special place" for her "special friend," Dirty Bird.
It's in the only "tidy" spot in her house!

And Dirty Bird makes sure that he takes care of Charm's books, too!
Her friendship is important to him. So, he makes sure
that he returns them to her in impeccable (im-PECK-able) condition!

That is why it is important to find something

that you like about everyone.

No one is perfect, and you can

be friends in spite of your differences.

So if you are tidy or not, you are still someone's friend!

THE END

About the Author Joel Brown

Joel resides in Decatur, Georgia and is an Atlanta native. He has two precious granddaughters. He loves to read bedtime stories to them. It was in these stories "Zoom-Boom" became alive. He uses his Christian beliefs to tell and share the many adventures of Zoom-Boom and his friends.

About the Illustrator Garrett Myers

Garrett resides in Albany, Georgia. He has been drawing since he was a little boy. He is gifted and talented and uses his gifts and talents to glorify God in all that he draws. He always reminds others that his drawings are creations from God, and his tools are His handiworks.

CPSIA information can be obtained
at www.ICGtesting.com
Printed in the USA
LVOW05s2113230616
493894LV00011B/107/P